C000076570

Short Stories

Sinister Tales
for Teens

Short Stories

Sinister Tales
for Teens

by

Dandi Palmer

Dodo Books

Copyright © Dandi Palmer
& Dodo Books 2017

First edition Dodo Books 2017

This is a work of fiction
and any resemblance to persons
living or dead is purely coincidental.

The author asserts the moral right to be identified as
the author of this work.

ISBN 978 1 906442 52 1

All rights reserved.
No part of this publication may be reproduced, stored in
a retrieval system, or transmitted, in any form or by any
means, electronic, mechanical, photocopying, recording
or otherwise, without the prior permission of the
publisher, nor be otherwise circulated in any form of
binding or cover other than that in which it is published
and without a similar condition being imposed on the
subsequent purchaser.

Stories

Tricardy, Dicardy and Boo
The trouble with triplets.

Clouds
*The clown from Hell - and another
from Heaven.*

The Terrible Toyshop
Wicked cure for delinquents.

The Smog
*Melt away into an alternative
dimension.*

Madam Phantasmagoria
Monsters on the golf course.

I'm on the Bus
Smartphones that swallow users.

Eyes in the Sky
An island under alien observation.

Game Over
Plug into an electronic dimension.

Butterflies
The chrysalis of hope.

Tricardy, Dicardy and Boo

The triplets' real names were George, Alan and Robert, but they insisted on being called Tricardy, Dicardy and Boo. Together they were known as the Trilobites because they were just a little weird; small identical brothers with the same thoughts apparently inhabiting three bodies. One of them would start a sentence and another finish it. It could be quite spooky. Other parents were overheard suggesting they were probably Midwich Cuckoos, though not within earshot of their proud mother and father.

Tricardy was the oldest by 30 minutes, and then came Dicardy, and lastly Boo, who only differed from his brothers by giggling a lot.

As they grew older (but not much larger), their birthdays became more problematic. Being identical, friends and relations were inclined to buy them exactly the same things. They should have known better and were always mortified by the way their gifts of soft toys, colouring books and Transformers were pushed into a cupboard and ignored. The boys much preferred to play with the building materials they somehow intimidated older friends to scavenge from skips. The influence the eight-year-olds had over other children was inexplicable to the adults who wondered what they were building.

Tricardy, Dicardy and Boo spent all their spare

1

time at the bottom of the garden constructing, what their parents assumed to be, a portal to welcome the aliens they claimed would shortly invade Earth.

While everyone else thought that the boys were odd, their parents assumed that it was normal for identical brothers to behave in exactly the same way until their mother started to become increasingly apprehensive about her sons' ability to perceive weird things no one else could see. It reached the point where Tricardy, Dicardy and Boo noticed the tension growing between their parents. It didn't worry them; they just carried on piling up planks, corrugated sheeting and wooden crates until they had created a rickety structure large enough to accommodate all three of them, Del the family dog, and any alien who might have dropped in. It was quite dangerous so one night their father dismantled the structure before it collapsed.

Tricardy, Dicardy and Boo expressed no annoyance at this act of vandalism, which the adults found more disconcerting than a triple tantrum.

During the ensuing argument between their parents, they overheard their mother tell their father that she had brief relationship with a young man at a motorway hotel over nine years previously. This confirmed their father's suspicion that the strange triplets were not his, though the boys couldn't understand why it made him so angry.

With a supreme effort, he overcame his outrage

2

and spent the following evenings sulking in the local pub.

In a few weeks life returned to normal; the boys building another dangerous structure and their mother behaving as though nothing was wrong.

Then Tricardy, Dicardy and Boo saw a handsome man arrive at the house. He hesitated at the front gate as though expecting Del, the elderly family spaniel with few remaining teeth, to attack him.

Even from the bay window, the triplets could see that the visitor's eyelashes were unusually long and dark, like theirs, and his skin had that yellowish pallor, which doctors had once thought was jaundice. He had not come in a taxi or car, and it was several miles from the nearest railway station. Perhaps he had landed in his spaceship?

The boys somehow knew the stranger had come to see them. They dashed out to meet him before he could reach the front door.

"Father is at work..." said Tricardy.

"And mother is ironing," said Dicardy.

"And they didn't speak to each other this morning," giggled Boo.

At the last comment the handsome man's eyes opened wide.

"Did you want to see her?" asked Tricardy.

"I can fetch her," offered Dicardy.

"But we don't really want to," giggled Boo.

"She's in a very bad mood."

"Why not talk to us instead?"

"Not many people talk to us."

"They say it's too confusing."

As the triplet's responses merged, it was easy to see why.

"I have come to see you," announced the man.

"Why?"

"We don't know who you are."

"I know who you are," the visitor told them.

"Who are we, then?"

"The same boy."

"How can we be the same boy?"

"It's complicated."

"That's what mother says."

"All the time."

"Are you sure you don't want to see her?"

The handsome man noticed a neighbour glowering suspiciously at him.

"Say nothing to her. I must go now. Meet me here at midnight without waking your parents."

And he strode away.

The triplets looked at each other. They didn't speak because they were all thinking the same thing.

Leaving the house at the dead of night was not easy. Slipping the bolts on the back door without waking Del was the most difficult part. If he woke up he would demand to go for a walk and howl if they refused to take him.

Del woke up.

Tricardy quickly fastened his lead and took the elderly spaniel with them.

The boys would never have done something this risky if the handsome man had not been so familiar. They instinctively knew that he would tell them something their parents had been keeping from them.

The stranger was waiting for the brothers on the other side of the front gate. He beckoned to them and they followed. Even if Del was virtually toothless, it was so dark he might have been ferocious for all the man knew.

Tricardy, Dicardy, and Boo, in their dressing gowns, and Del, anticipating a romp on the heath, reached the hollow where children lit bonfires and roasted potatoes. Even in the moonlight the place seemed familiar until the spaniel, which had been running ahead of them, suddenly stopped at the sight of a dome pulsing with a dull glow. It was higher than the garden shed, but concealed from the nearby houses by a stand of trees. As the triplets approached, the pulsing of the light increased as though it recognised them.

Tricardy was tempted to reach out and touch its surface. "Are you an alien?"

Dicardy joined him. "And experiment on humans?"

"We wouldn't like that," giggled Boo, placing his hands on the dome. "It feels really funny - like lots of ants crawling on my skin."

"It will do you no harm," the handsome man reassured them.

"That's what adults say when they know it will..."

"But we never listen to them..."

"But we trust you. You have long eyelashes, like ours."

"And are yellow."

The stranger at last explained. "About nine years ago something dreadful - and quite wonderful - happened. It was because of me you came into being."

"We know how that's done."

"Mostly."

"Adults do very silly things," Boo giggled.

"When I met your mother I had never encountered a human so attractive before. She did not realise who I really was. I should have known better than to make love to her and been aware of what could happen. The genetic compatibility to create a child is only temporary and very limited."

The triplets, not understanding a word, were now convinced he came from another planet.

"Who are you?" asked Tricardy.

"You have to tell us before we listen to you."

"Even if that is very silly as well."

The handsome man stood against the dome, silhouetted by its glow. "We are your father. I am Jepat, Colos and Varin."

As he spoke his silhouette divided into three

parts.

"My name is Jepat," said one.

"Mine is Colos," said another.

"And I am Varin," explained the last. "Together we are one."

The triplets were too astonished to say anything.

"On this world you should also be one. The trinity of being can only exist on my planet."

Each manifestation of their true father reached out to the equivalent of his corresponding son. Tricardy, Dicardy and Boo took the offered hands and grasped them. As they did so the triplets' bodies merged and became one sturdy young boy.

Jepat, Colos and Varin reverted to the good-looking man who had helped them make sense of their existence.

The children who had been christened George, Alan and Robert never saw him again. He may have solved the conundrum of who they actually were, but not how their mother was going to explain the triplet's disappearance to family, friends and neighbours and arrival of a new son.

At least her husband was more inclined to accept the tall, handsome child as his, unlike the tiny, irksome trio forever finishing each others sentences and building contraptions to welcome aliens.

Clouds

There was an elephant, and then a witch on a broom.

Sunita waved to them as they scudded by and was sure the clouds responded by rolling and swirling as she willed them into different shapes.

Her father found this preoccupation with cumulus and cirrus amusing, but then he found most things amusing, especially children.

As Sunita's mother had died when she was born she had never known what it was like to have two parents, unlike most of her friends, and sometimes wished that her father would remarry. Joyce in the corner shop was rather nice, and her father liked Joyce, but she was twice his age and her husband probably wouldn't have agreed.

Perhaps Sunita could conjure up a beautiful woman in the clouds to come down and fill that empty space there seemed to be in the house when the surgery closed. Dr Ranjit was constantly busy, but always found time for his imaginative daughter. They lived above his surgery so she was never alone when it was open and liked to chat to the patients in the waiting room. Some of the elderly ones told her tales from their childhood, when there were no doctors unless you were wealthy enough to pay for them. One small boy who was seriously ill would not have survived if he had been born then. Sunita was particularly fond of him because he never complained or cried. Every week Simon, always carrying an old, much-loved yellow teddy bear with a pink bowtie, would visit her father for a regular check-up.

One day when he arrived for his appointment he was very tearful. His mother explained that his teddy bear had mysteriously disappeared. Later, when he could not hear, she told Sunita that the toy had to be hidden away because it posed an infection risk. Poor Simon was inconsolable however much she tried to comfort him. To Sunita it seemed so unfair that the teddy that kept the seriously ill child content had to be the very thing that could kill him. His mother had tried to find another just like it, scouring everywhere from the high street to online retailers. But the bear was unique, custom-made for a great aunt who had passed it down through the family. Small wonder it might have carried a century's catalogue of infections.

That evening Sunita dejectedly sat in the garden as the sun went down and watched the round, yellow cumulus about to pass over the radiant globe. It was bubble-shaped, so she willed the cloud to take the shape of Simon's teddy bear and a wispy swirl of red cirrus untie itself from the sunset to settle at the bear's neck in the shape of a large pink bow.

Sunita leapt up and clapped her hands with joy. Her father, working in the sun lounge, wondered what had so delighted her and came out to see a large, yellow shape gently floating down from the sky.

Dr Ranjit had seen many things and, though he would not have declared it too loudly to some patients, believed in the multitude of gods that exist-ed in all living creatures. This was so remarkable he wondered if his young daughter could be one of those deities. Anyone else, seeing the large yellow bear with the pink bowtie sitting on the lawn by the pots of geraniums, would have suspected it was a trick. But Dr Ranjit knew his daughter. There was not a devious gene in her body.

Just to be convinced that he was not seeing things and the original bear, which should have been well hidden, had not made an unexpected reappearance after a good shampoo, he took it into his surgery and plucked samples from its fur to send away for analysis. When the results came back they confirmed that there was no trace of any infection which could harm Simon; in fact, it possessed antibacterial properties to prevent it.

Sunita wrapped the bear and put it in a box, which she presented to the young patient the next time he came for his check-up, and handed the proof of its clean bill of health to his mother. From then on the toddler began to grow stronger. Soon Simon only needed to be examined once a month.

Someone dressed like an evil clown had been terrorising the children at Sunita's school as they left the gates, so most parents waited outside for them. Others went home in groups. Jerry, Dr Ranjit's receptionist, usually collected Sunita after locking the waiting room to ensure she did not have to come back alone.

The clown had not harmed anyone, but the police did not want to take the chance he would and had an officer in uniform standing by until everyone had left.

One afternoon Jerry's car was involved in a minor collision on the way to the school, which meant he had to exchange details with the other driver and was delayed. Sunita had forgotten her mobile phone again and he was unable to contact her. By the time he arrived, the school gates were closed so Jerry assumed that Sunita and her friend, Tracey, had decided to return home together.

The walk through a lane to the other side of the estate was almost a mile. Sunita and Tracy were halfway home when the creepy clown wearing make-up straight out of a horror film jumped out in front of them.

He moved menacingly towards the girls.

Tracy screamed.

That was what he wanted to hear and raised his white-gloved hands as though about to attack them.

But Sunita was angry. Any adult who needed to scare schoolchildren was a bully and a coward. He needed to be taught a lesson.

In reply, she raised her hands to the sky.

The clouds above churned with stormy malice.

The clown didn't notice them and found Sunita's defiance amusing - the girl should have been terrified, not challenging him. The bully felt protected by his vile make up. Knowing he could not be recognised, the clown took out a baseball bat which had been hidden by his baggy jacket.

Tracy was now hysterical. This terror of the school gates had never threatened to harm any of the pupils before, but out here in the deserted lane there was no one to stop him.

The malicious clown raised the weapon to strike Sunita and ensure she never dared confront a bully again.

Then he suddenly stopped and stared.

Behind the girls, silently pounding towards him, was a monstrous clown twice his height and ten times as scary. The giant was surrounded by an unearthly glow and his wide mouth, filled with sharp teeth, wore a scowl that could have curdled milk.

The other clown suddenly felt very small and scared. He dropped the baseball bat and ran off, screeching in terror.

Tracy stopped panicking, wondering what had frightened off their attacker. Before she could turn, the huge clown had dispersed back into the sky. Minutes later, Jerry's car with its buckled fender pulled up beside them just in time to see the clown disappearing into the distance. He phoned the police and gave them the exact location.

The clown was not caught, but never bothered the pupils of Sunita's school again.

The Terrible Toyshop

It was the dead of night in the High Street.

Tina, Trog and Jamie knew where the CCTV cameras were pointing and how to avoid them. Despite causing mayhem in the small town, they had not been caught yet.

The more disruptive troublemakers they used to steer clear of had disappeared weeks ago. Now the three teenagers had the town to themselves.

The porch of the small shop offered plenty of cover, and the glass-fronted door had only one draw bolt. It would be easy to break into, so there was probably nothing worth stealing inside. They could still trash the place, though. That's what they were best at; the worst nightmare of all shopkeepers who opened up in the morning to discover their valuable stock destroyed. If Tina, Trog and Jamie just stole what they could carry it would have been understandable, but they only did it to inflict grief on others. It gave them a feeling of control in an increasingly complicated world.

Tina broke the stained-glass panel in the door and reached through to open the single bolt securing it. There was no alarm and the inside of the shop was lit by a safety light, so she beckoned Trog and Jamie to follow her in.

As they explored, the teenagers became aware

that they were being watched. Malevolent glass eyes were turning to follow their every movement.

The young delinquents were terrified and would have dashed back out if a deadlock on the door hadn't turned with a resounding 'clunk' and shut them inside. There was no key to open it and the broken glass panel too small to escape through.

They were trapped.

The only way out was through a small door at the rear of the shop.

One pair of marble-sized glass eyes belonged to a life-sized, menacing clown.

This began looming from the shadows towards them.

Panicking, Tina, Trog and Jamie tripped over each other to escape through the door.

When they were on the other side of it there was no one to hear the young people scream.

The shelves of the newly-opened Victorian toyshop were filled with dolls wearing thin-lipped smiles on their ceramic faces, glove puppets of strange animals, and monkeys which could jump up and down on a stick. At centre of the shop was a merry-go-round of prancing ponies, unicorns and a flying pig.

In this mysterious shop the rocking horse rocked without being touched, the ballerina on the music box whirled to its trill tune without needing a turn of the key, and the merry-go-round waltzed round and round at the slightest draft. The local newspaper had dismissed it as electronic trickery because the proprietor refused to be interviewed by one of their reporters.

The occasional customer came in to stand and marvel, yet no one purchased a toy for their children. There was something too sinister about these playthings to inflict on a modern infant. It was more like an outlet for grandmothers who disliked technology's gadgets and their grandchildren. Toys that had to be pushed, pulled or wound up should have thrilled many infants, but the sinister, glass-eyed ones displayed in this toyshop were more likely to make them burst into tears.

So how did this shop make any money? Did it carry out all its business online? Were its customers wealthy collectors? None of the toys were priced and there was no proprietor to purchase them from. The antiquated till with yellowed keys looked as though it had not been used for a hundred years and its float was probably in shillings, pennies and farthings. With the lack of security it should have been a shoplifter's paradise, but the menacing ambience of the place was a deterrent in itself. And then there was the way the toyshop had appeared overnight, fully stocked, in the small property between the local supermarket and newsagent. The premises had been empty for years and both outlets had tried to purchase it, but the agent told them that the leaseholder was holding it in reserve for when the community needed it most.

One young mother reported the toyshop to the police for scaring her children. But they had other things to worry about. Local teenagers had been disappearing. All of them were troublemakers and it was assumed that they were hiding to avoid being charged with criminal behaviour. Now so many had gone missing it could no longer be ignored, however glad law enforcement was to see the back of them.

The local newspaper was also more interested in the lost tearaways than wasting column space on the strange toyshop. As that was so low on their list, Coral, an aspiring reporter, decided that this would be a good qualification project for her course on journalism. Her writing skills were exemplary and interviewing techniques remarkable for a 15-year-old. All she needed now was an A plus pass for investigative reporting.

Coral checked in the wardrobe mirror that she looked the part before setting out. It was essential to appear professional and five years older.

Was her skirt too short, too tight or the wrong colour?

Should she wear lipstick and mascara, or tie up her box braids?

Heels, trainers or sensible flat shoes?

If she had stood and thought about it any longer she would have never left the house, and it was a good mile walk to the town centre. So flat, sensible shoes it was - the trainers were far too shabby anyway.

When Coral reached the toyshop it seemed different, but she couldn't work out what had changed since she last went past. The clown in the stained-glass door panel looked larger - though that wasn't possible when the door was still the same size... and its smile had turned into a scowl.

Shrugging off the uneasy feeling, Coral pushed the door open. The bell rang resoundingly on its coiled spring and she felt the glass eyes of the toys gazing at her. At this point her less determined friends would have quickly left. This teenager was made of sterner stuff though, and strode to the mysterious merry-go-round, trying not to wonder what had set it in motion.

Another sinister clown in its cabinet cackled insanely, daring her to put a coin in its slot. The teenager refused to be intimidated and explored the small shop of scary toys until she came to an alcove concealed by a faded maroon curtain. Coral drew it aside to find a child-sized door. Perhaps the proprietor was in the parlour on the other side, creating another magical invention?

This was Alice in Wonderland territory. Should the aspiring reporter go in and eat the cake or drink the potion which would make her the height of the Eiffel Tower or size of a gerbil and be rewarded with the story that would secure her career? Having seen what cannabis did to people, there was no chance of that.

But there was no harm in peering inside, so Coral lifted the latch. It was not the door to a parlour.

It really was Wonderland.

Despite its Victorian ambience, this world lacked Lewis Carroll's dreamlike reassurance.

Coral mustered all her confidence and entered a place inhabited by life-sized toys that giggled manically or frantically waved as she passed by.

They were all horribly real.

The ballerina pivoting on the huge music box did so as though she desperately wanted to escape. The monkey on the stick was more boy than simian, contorted into awkward movements against his will, and other huge, stuffed toys flapped their boneless arms as if trying to break out of their stitches.

It was quite terrifying.

Passing the monstrous toys as fast as she could, Coral reached the imposing roundabout at the centre of this weird playground. It was a life-sized version of the replica in the shop and the only exhibit not moving, as though waiting for the next visitor gullible enough to get onto one of its sinister looking mounts. Even if she had been tempted, the evil squint of the flying pig was deterrent enough.

The aspiring reporter pulled out her camera.

She was recording the collection of nightmare

toys when a forbidding figure dressed in a long black skirt with the sheen of a raven's wing glided towards her. Her beauty was spoilt by - what the teenager thought was - a wicked expression. This was hardly the benign toymaker the teenager had hoped to meet; more vampire than mortal craftworker.

"Well now, what are you doing here, little one?"

Although the woman was floating threateningly above her, Coral resented being spoken down to as though she was an infant. "I might ask you the same thing?"

"I am the Toymaker, and merely passing through."

"To do what, and for how long?"

"To fulfil a popular public service, which will last as long as it takes."

Coral had already guessed what that - somewhat disturbing - public service was. "There are probably laws against using a toyshop to trap badly-behaved teenagers. Just what have you done to them?"

The sinister woman was taken back by her acuity and floated down to look her in the eye. "Well aren't you the clever one. Worked it out without having to ask."

"So this is what you call a public service? Trapping young people my age and turning them into toys?"

"Oh, it won't be forever, just until they learn how to behave themselves."

However much Coral disapproved of delinquent behaviour in her peer group, it was difficult to believe that they deserved to be turned into animatronics and stuffed dolls. "And I suppose you are the judge of when that will be?"

"No, not at all. As soon as they are genuinely sorry, they will automatically be released."

"You are aware their parents must be going out of their minds with worry, aren't you?"

"Well of course they aren't. Their children wouldn't have turned out this way if they had cared enough to bring them up properly. And time in the real world is a mere blink of the eyelid. They can stay here for as long as it takes, but return to whatever point in time they choose."

"I suppose you supply packed lunches and the fare to start new lives in the Andromeda Galaxy as well?"

Coral was obviously being sarcastic. She didn't expect the sinister woman to admit, "If that's what they need to be free of their old ways, certainly."

Coral glanced at her camera and saw that it hadn't recorded one image. It was enough to make her wonder if she wasn't imagining it all. One glance at the unguarded expression of the Toymaker told her that was what she had been counting on it. A promising student damned by the label of fantasist would be no threat to her 'public service'.

"I'm still not leaving without a story," Coral

declared defiantly.

There was not much the woman could do about that. This tough teenager was totally unlike the others she dealt with. She was intelligent.

"What sort of story?"

"A good exposé that can be backed up by facts."

"Oh, you are a little madam, aren't you?"

"You'd better believe it."

Coral's main fault was ambition. That was no reason to turn her into one of the terrible toys.

The Toymaker decided to give her what she wanted, and at the same time put to rest one of her failures. "Some while ago a couple of youths killed a young boy for fun. Unfortunately I cannot be in all places at once and watch every miscreant but, had I been paying attention at the time, I could have prevented the murder by including them in one of my 'corrective' facilities before they committed it. They got away with it, buried the child's body, and went on to have the fulfilled lives they had robbed him of. The police and boy's parents have been searching for him ever since."

Coral was immediately enthused. "Tell me who they were?"

"Not so fast, little one. Before dying, consumed with remorse at helping to cover up what his son had done, a father of one of the youths wrote a letter. It reveals where boy's body was buried. In the grave is enough forensic evidence to convict the perpetrators."

"Why not just tell me who his murderers were?"

"Don't be foolish. If you approached them - as you well know - you could be killed as well, and your ambition to be a reporter will end there. I will tell you where you can find this sealed letter. Research the details, write up the story, and then take what you find out to the police."

It was an offer Coral could not refuse. Any story about the phantom toyshop would destroy her career before it started. "How can I trust you?"

"Look at your phone."

Coral saw a text message arrive. It gave instructions on how to contact the executrix handling the estate and papers of the father in question. How Coral persuaded her to surrender the letter would be up to her.

This gave the budding journalist an idea. "We couldn't come to some arrangement about you supplying me with more stories, could we?"

"Don't push it, kid."

The Toymaker's black gown folded about her like raven wings and the next second Coral was standing in the high street outside the toyshop. The front was now boarded up with a TO LET sign nailed above it.

Learning about the youths who murdered a child for fun tended to dampen any empathy Coral had for the teenagers trapped by its last nightmare proprietor.

Normality was restored by the shoppers spilling

out of the supermarket with loaded trolleys on one side, and customers leaving the newsagents with their cigarettes and newspapers on the other. Would any one of them have believed that the toyshop between the two outlets had trapped several young tearaways who had been disrupting the life of the neighbourhood? And would they have particularly cared?

Coral went to the park to check out the story in the text and plot her next move. According to news reports of the time, the murder had been true. Traces of tissue and blood had been found but, as the Toymaker had told her, no body or incriminating evidence. It was more than ambition which made her feel obliged to pursue the story. The bereaved parents needed to know where their child was. The fact the culprits were now adults, probably with families of their own, was an injustice too far. Coral didn't know it at the time, but this was the moment her life was set on course as a crusading journalist.

The budding reporter closed her smartphone and strolled around the lake to think. The ducks were squabbling and trying to beat the pigeons to chunks of bread tossed by children. The park was peaceful without rowdy clusters of young people congregating to drink cider and intimidate passers-by. It was such a relief to be able to walk from one end of it to the other without some lewd comment or the risk of being mown down by a mountain bike.

The story of the phantom toyshop was absurd anyway. The only things on her camera were snapshots of her parents in a loving embrace when they thought the younger children weren't watching and a beautiful rainbow over the gasometers, which had been irresistible.

Thank goodness there was still some beauty in the world.

The Smog

It was another of those dank, late October afternoons when the sun, however hard it tried, could not penetrate the dense smog. Five miles away in the countryside the fields were radiant with its autumn rays.

In town, it soon wouldn't be possible for Oswald to see three feet in front of him, let alone to the end of the back-to-back terrace, so he had been allowed out of classes early.

As soon as he arrived home and unloaded his satchel, he left to collect his five-year-old sister from infant school two streets away. During the summer Alice would have been quite happy to come back with her two older friends. But the smog altered everything. The traffic slowed to a crawl and workers leaving the factory, on which the local economy depended, found it quicker to walk than wait for a bus. The upper decks of the Routemasters already reeked of stale tobacco smoke and damp gabardine and the sulphuric smog rolled in through the open platforms.

When Oswald reached the school, the infants had been kept inside until someone arrived to collect them. The smog was growing thicker. Everyone knew that it was unhealthy to breathe in, but it was the only air they had outside their homes.

Alice was in a petulant mood; even her favourite pastime of making plasticine people had not improved it. When they got home she wanted Oswald to read her a book, despite knowing that he had to collect the groceries before the shop closed and she wouldn't get tea until the tin of pineapple slices and loaf of bread arrived.

As their mother was busy with the laundry, Oswald brought out the doll's house to occupy his young sister until he came back.

He hated having to shop in this weather. The local grocer was half a mile away and on fine days there was the shortcut across Memorial Park. The thick smog made that impossible. He would have to walk around it, hearing the distant quacking of disgruntled ducks who dare not take off for fear of flying into a tree.

It had gone 6 o'clock when Oswald started his journey back with a basket full of groceries. The weight of the tins and potatoes made the 14-year-old's arms ache, and the wicker scratched his legs because he couldn't lift it any higher. It was no use; as he reached the bench by the park he had to rest.

The headlights of a slowly passing car penetrated the gloom, picking out a shape wending its confused way about the lawn on the other side of the railing. Oswald wondered what anyone could be doing there when it was difficult to see very far in front of you. Perhaps the man was up to no good, but he seemed to be disorientated, lurching this way and that as though looking for some way out.

Oswald went to the park's gate and took a few steps in to see if someone needed help. As he got closer he recognised the work clothes of a neighbour. "Mr Brown! Mr Brown! Are you all right?"

There was no reply and Oswald could see... he wasn't quite sure what. It was certainly Mr Brown's face, but it wore a strange expression.

Dennis Brown was a fit man in his thirties with a large family. He shouldn't have lost his way and be wandering about Memorial Park. When the smog was this bad, workers were allowed to leave early instead of completing their eight to six o'clock shift. So why wasn't Mr Brown at home?

He briefly recognised Oswald and tried to tell him something.

Then an eerie glow enveloped the neighbour.

The teenager recoiled in horror as Dennis Brown's body dissolved into the light until nothing recognisable remained.

Oswald could not recall if he screamed, or remember snatching up the basket of groceries and running for dear life to the police station. It was twice the distance from his home and he had no idea how he reached it so quickly.

The desk sergeant took some time to calm down the 14-year-old, and it was only after a mug of tea and cigarette he was able to describe what he had seen. Had Oswald been thinking straight he would have wondered why his outpouring was taken so seriously. What he had witnessed must have been impossible.

As his parents didn't have a telephone, the teenager and the basket of groceries were driven back home to his increasingly anxious family. The only one unconcerned was Alice, resentful that he had spent so long bringing home her tea.

Oswald later overheard a rumour that Dennis Brown had been in Memorial Park to look for his eldest son's football which had been kicked over the railings on the way home from school. His wife never forgave herself for asking him to go and find it.

Oswald heard no more about the incident. A collection was made to help Mrs Brown pay the rent arrears so the family was not evicted. Dennis Brown was eventually declared legally dead so she was able to collect a widow's pension.

It was only much later that Oswald learnt of other people disappearing in Memorial Park. He was probably the only one to be close to someone when they had been swallowed by the smog. The police recorded all of them as missing persons.

Once the Clean Air Act had been passed, there was no more smog. The late autumn skies were once more visible and that oily coating which smothered everything no longer had to be scrubbed away. Now it was left to tobacco and traffic pollution to destroy people's health.

Oswald and Alice grew apart after he left to join the Navy and she married a Dutchman.

They did not meet again until he was well into his seventies. Oswald frequently told his grandchildren about the neighbour that had melted in the park. Alice told hers that her brother was delusional and used to see things, and it was a wonder the Navy accepted him.

When they did eventually meet, they hardly recognised each other.

Oswald never again entered Memorial Park, despite coming back to his home town to retire. So he didn't see the infants' playground filled with swings, roundabouts, slides, and climbing frames. He also didn't hear the accounts of dog walkers claiming to have seen phantom shapes in the early evening spring mists.

One young woman was intrigued by the reports, even if her superiors weren't. PC Sarah Solomons had recently joined the police force. As a child she had heard about the disappearances in the smog and wondered then why the mystery had never been solved, not thinking for one moment that she would be the one to attempt it because no one else seemed interested.

With access to the police database she was able to

read the reports about the people who went missing in the smog of the 1950s. Searching the history of Memorial Park did invite rebukes from more senior officers who told her to stop wasting time. That just made PC Solomons determined to do it when off duty as she had at least one lead to follow. Oswald was the only person to actually see someone dissolve away and it didn't take long to track him down.

Despite 57 years passing since Dennis Brown melted from sight, it was almost a relief for that knock on the door to announce someone had, at last, begun to take his experience seriously. Sarah Solomons may have been a lowly PC, but she suspected that the reappearance of the phantoms in Memorial Park had something to do with Oswald. He wasn't enthusiastic about her theory, but believed the young woman deserved promotion if she managed to solve the mystery that had baffled the police force of his day.

After all those years, he was persuaded to return to Memorial Park.

In the setting spring sun it was light years away from the sinister, smog-filled place he remembered. Daffodils bloomed in the borders and the sticky buds of chestnut were preparing to burst open. Squirrels were busy building drays for new broods and birds plucked fur from the combings of someone's German shepherd to line their nests. The 72-year-old Oswald barely recognised the tidy, re-landscaped Memorial

Park. Surely no phantom or malevolent force would dare intrude here.

"The sightings are usually about this time, just as the sun is about to set," PC Solomons explained. "The eyewitnesses claimed it was as though these ghosts were reaching out from a distant portal into this world, and always in the same place."

Oswald was incredulous. "And you wonder whether we should invite them in?"

"What harm could there be if they really do exist? There are things in this Universe beyond the comprehension of the human mind; it doesn't mean they're evil."

It was obvious the young woman not only had the optimism of youth, but another theory which had been dismissed by her superiors as fantasy. Oswald was keen to hear it. Even after a lifetime, the disappearance of Dennis Brown remained horrific. Knowing what had happened to him might help alleviate the memory.

"There could be a merging with another dimension which briefly causes an overlap in time, just long enough for those unsuspecting souls to have fallen through it."

Her conjecture seemed plausible to Oswald who had come across many strange things, especially when he had been in the Navy.

"Can you remember exactly where it happened?" PC Solomons pointed to the flowerbed near the main entrance where the dog walkers had seen the phantoms. "Recent reports say it was somewhere about there."

"Must have been. I didn't go any further into the park." Oswald prodded the flowerbed's border of late crocuses with his walking stick. "This was just grass back then."

The setting sun caught the colours in the pale petals and turned them flame red. Old man and young woman shuddered as they sensed a strange rift in reality.

The last shaft of sunlight picked out a ghostly portal.

Without thinking, Oswald called out, "Mr Brown... are you there?" hardly expecting a response.

Then something began to materialise.

The shadow of the man he had seen disappear over 50 years before was barely visible and his words echoed from a different dimension.

"Hello Oswald. We have been waiting for you."

The old man's blood ran cold. It was just as well he had a strong heart.

"Why? What do you want with me?"

"We need people like you to join us. Don't be alarmed. Here you will become young again and never age. Why wouldn't you want to cross over?"

Oswald was on the verge of panic. "But I've got a family! And you had a family, Dennis Brown!"

"But you must come! Join our family here and

live forever!"

As the phantom reached out to pull him though the rip in time, a brief window into a nightmarish world opened.

Oswald was frozen in horror and powerless to resist, despite his determination not to go. He was being dragged through the portal into a volcanic world full of fire and conflict. Young men like Dennis Brown were being slaughtered and maimed, only to rise up and start fighting again in an alien dimension of never-ending carnage. It was so terrible Oswald couldn't believe that the mild-mannered neighbour had become one of these murderous psychopaths. But there he was, grasping his arm with every intention of turning him into one of them.

Oswald preferred to die a natural death, not one over and over again on the battlefields of an alien world. He tried to pull back, but was not strong enough.

Just as he could no longer resist something with superhuman strength snatched Oswald back. He toppled on top of them into the crocuses.

The dreadful portal immediately closed.

PC Solomons helped him up. "Sorry about that, but you were starting to disappear. You okay?"

Oswald managed to catch his breath.

"Did you see any of that?"

"Enough to know that some alien contacts are probably not such a good idea."

"I don't want to live forever. It's not natural. I would have thought a fit young woman like you would be a better candidate for cannon fodder. Why weren't you pulled through instead?"

"You didn't know, did you?"

"Know what?"

"All the people who disappeared through that portal were male. Women and girls had been in the same place and walked right past it. They were ignored. At least we now know what all those blokes were needed for."

"Pity no one will ever believe us."

Madam Phantasmagoria

Joey loved to wear pink since the age of three. When he was seven he wanted to be called Peony. Despite being an engaging and exceptionally intelligent boy, at school he was teased by pupils and teachers alike.

He learnt at a young age that jealousy and intolerance are a toxic mix.

Joey's parents were no more enlightened and told him to stop pretending to be a girl. Most others with a child this talented would have taken him to a consultant in transgender matters instead. But they lived in a village where gossip dictated a person's status on the community ladder and his parents had aspirations beyond their bank balance.

So Joey was bullied into cross-country runs and football training after school to toughen him up. Because his parents were too occupied with their social life to keep an eye on their son, the football coach allowed him to spend the time with Robyn, the local herbalist. A reluctant, uncompetitive player was of little use to the team, and the young boy's much older friend was locally regarded with respect verging on awe. While they sipped her delicious cordials, she was happy to discuss with Joey matters which were beyond others in his age group.

Rumour had it that Robyn was a witch with mysterious powers. Nobody was sure what they were, any more than they knew where her heavy European accent came from. The herbalist had lived in her cottage for as long as the oldest inhabitant, Aggie, could remember. Though, as she spent most of her time in the Fox and Falcon drinking gin and tonic, anything she recalled was taken with a pinch of salt. Her claim that the herbalist had belonged to a French travelling circus whose performers sometimes dropped by to visit her cottage was also dismissed as alcoholic rambling. And then there were the potions: as these were more effective than most medicines the doctor prescribed, coupled with her supposed supernatural abilities, no one questioned Robyn's friendship with Joey.

That didn't stop the teasing, though.

When he joined the senior school it became worse. However much Joey now tried to conceal his past innocent desire to be a girl, it pursued him. He was taunted mercilessly and called Peony by everyone from the moment he got on the bus in the morning until he left it in the afternoon. Three boys in particular, Will, Stuart and John, teamed up to make his life a misery. The only relief from that and the disapproval of his parents were the secret visits to Robyn. She had a remarkable wardrobe of luxurious costumes in her spare bedroom. With these and a few minor adjustments, Joey enjoyed being transformed into an astonishing young woman, truly an attractive adolescent about to blossom into a Peony.

These secret visits would have continued if Will,

the leader of the gang who bullied him, had not discovered what was happening. He managed to snap a couple of pictures of Joey dressed as a woman. These he posted online to ensure they spread like wildfire. Joey's parents, believing they had dealt with their son's delusion about his gender, were furious.

After several weeks of increasing abuse, Joey, aged 12, disappeared.

The farmland and woods surrounding the village were searched.

No trace of him was ever found.

Parents, police and teachers all thought the same thing, though few dare admit that it was hardly surprising the boy had run away.

To escape the embarrassment, his parents moved to the small villa they had bought in Spain. Two years later its foundations shifted and the property collapsed. Being the one thing they had not thought to insure against, they ended up living in a block of flats where no one spoke English.

Without the distraction of Joey to torment, Will, Stuart and John focussed their attentions on a business course. Financial acumen presented far more opportunities to persecute people out there in the big, wide world.

After the three qualified and left university, Will's father raised the capital to enable them to form a property company, Wolf Enterprises. He had not expected his son to return to their home village with

Stuart and John and start buying it up to sell as second homes for wealthy city dwellers. Matters were made even worse when the family house had to be sold to cover the father's rash investment in a son he had not recognised to be a greedy bully until it was too late.

Many local residents had their rents tripled by Wolf Enterprises, which had bought their leases, and they could no longer afford to live in their picturesque corner of the countryside. The village school was closed for lack of pupils and the small high street became virtually deserted until the weekends when the expensive new restaurant and specialist shops opened for the wealthy newcomers. After effectively destroying the community, this group of enterprising young men went on to buy the common from the impoverished parish council to create a golf course. The manor house once owned by the squire became an exclusive hotel, and even the ducks were evicted from the village pond, which was relegated to a hazard on the fifteenth hole of the golf course.

Those remaining locals found themselves second class citizens living in an elite community of bankers and businessman who used it as a retreat from the city treadmill of making exorbitant amounts of money. Many who had mocked Joey, along with Will, Stuart and John, saw it as a judgement for tormenting the boy. Will's father regretted his son's behaviour most of all and, with the few resources he had left, tried to find out what had happened to the pupil everyone called Peony, though without success. The only person who might have been able to answer that was the herbalist.

As the world about Robyn was reduced to a playground for the rich, she continued to potter around her smallholding growing herbs, grinding potions, and chuckling to herself. Only one or two people knew what amused her, including the vicar, who in the past had needed to fend off the insistence of parishioners that he denounce her as a witch. Those who didn't know believed it was because Wolf Enterprises could not buy her out. The intimidating letters they sent Robyn were responded to by an expensive lawyer by return of post. So they left her alone, secure in her cottage and smallholding of fruit trees, vegetable plots and herbs, not realising how much things were about to change.

Just as the property company's investments were on the cusp of paying dividends to its shareholders, the phantoms began to appear.

The first one was benign; a graceful woman in white magically gliding across the golf course fairway at the dead of night, only observed by the local poacher and groundsmen coming home from the Fox and Falcon. The sighting was put down to inebriation, one of the myths the late, much-missed Aggie would have dreamt up in the pub's snug.

But then the monster arrived. No imagination,

however addled or senile, could have conjured up this nightmarish creature.

Just as the light was fading and the last golfers were making their ways back to the clubhouse, the terrifying apparition loomed out of the trees and bore down on the men. (It was always men, as women were not welcome on the sacrosanct fairways. Wolf Enterprises had ensured that it remained one of the club's best selling points.) One moment nebulous, the next horrifyingly real, the shape-shifting bugaboo insinuated its malevolent way through carefully arranged copses and over immaculately manicured fairways like a hideous amoeba. One moment it was a fiery dragon in front of them, the next a monstrous serpent uncoiling from deep bunkers.

One of the golfers had a minor stroke, and another fell into a fit of hysteria that could only be calmed by a powerful sedative from paramedics.

Understandably no one thought to record the creature on their mobiles - they were running too fast - which didn't stop the news of its appearance travelling like wildfire.

The village was invaded by ghost hunters, dragon slayers, and odd cults formed on the spur of the moment in Facebook. Will, Stuart, and John's company was obliged to launch an expensive campaign to counter the rumours and pay a security company to stop the monster hunters from gatecrashing their precious real estate. However many felt the need to be frightened out of their wits by a hideous phantom (it was more exhilarating than pursuing Pokémon) the city well-to-do who had ruined the heart of the village were not so keen. The value of their property began to plummet.

The golf course's groundsmen were ordered out with guns, ready for the bugaboo's next appearance. But this wasn't in their job description and only Wolf Enterprises' threats of instant dismissal persuaded them to confront the monster. Few of them were local and as soon as the evil-eyed, fire-breathing serpent lunged out of the trees towards them, they regretted ever coming to the village. Some stood their ground and discharged round after round. But the bullets went straight through the creature. Not even a steady wage could convince the men that it was worth confronting this every evening. Enough was enough. They fled in terror to find golf courses without resident monsters.

The police were not interested. There was nothing unusual about inebriated, overweight men having medical emergencies during a game of golf. Resources were not going to be wasted on what was most likely a practical joke when farm machinery was being stolen and there were the dens of cannabis growers to raid. Given the social standing of the members of the golf club who had encountered the terrifying creatures, they resented the offhand way the local constabulary dismissed their complaints. Not only did the apparition trigger heart attacks, it had disrupted their golf and lowered the value of their properties.

Then the phantoms started to appear in the new cul-de-sacs where Wolf Enterprises had sunk some of the capital Will's father had raised to build mansions for the wealthy. These spectres were even more horrific.

The workmen immediately downed tools on construction work. There was plenty of employment in other parts of the country, and as the company's shares begun to plummet the builders knew the mansions would never be completed.

Will, Stuart and John had to do something. But how could they get rid of a phantom?

The local vicar, having had most of his original flock replaced by weekend Christians more interested in being seen in Church than following the teachings of Jesus, had no intention of exorcising the spectres. Also, by the way he held secret meetings with Robyn and several other villagers in his vestry, he probably knew more about the hauntings than he was prepared to admit. The comings and goings through the cemetery at the dead of night would have gone unnoticed if the suspicions of Ray, the community constable, had not become suspicious.

One evening, before watching his favourite cooking competition on TV, he hid behind a Victorian tombstone to see what was going on.

Fortunately he had set his programme to record,

because it was well past ten before members of the clandestine meeting began to arrive. Some of them were villagers and others complete strangers. One was Will's father, the man who had risked penury to fund his son's business. On arrival they all entered the outside door to the crypt which had historically been used as the village's storage space. Everything from home-made jam for summer bazaars to cement mixers used to repair the crumbling foundations had been down there at some time or another. Ray could just make out projectors and other electronic equipment being taken in. He thought that it was an odd time and place to have a film show, but that was because he would never be a detective, otherwise he might have worked out what was really going on. But a comfortable armchair and cholesterol rich dinner waited in his warm sitting room. If the professional coppers weren't interested, why should he be bothered? So, curiosity satisfied, he went home.

If he had waited a little longer he might have seen that huge, coffin-sized box being eased through the crypt's narrow entrance.

Within a few weeks most of the wealthy newcomers had decided their weekend retreats were anything but restful and flocked back to the relative peace and quiet of the City and its suburbs. There at least, most horrors were generated on stock market screens. And for the weird and wonderful they were more inclined to visit the spectacular performances of the new phenomenon, a French illusionist who could create exquisite visions able to confound the most hardened disbelievers in magic. Watching her was preferable to being pursued across a golf course by nightmare creatures more usually conjured up by drug abuse. At least that brief experience in the village had persuaded many of them to give up the habit. It was far more liberating to drool over the tall, elegant woman who could fill the stage with bubbles that burst into glittering confetti, which in turn became a cloud of iridescent butterflies. Even other seasoned magicians had no idea how she did it, though many held secret debates to try and work it out. Her talent could have only come from a deep heritage of experience, most likely circus in origin. But everything about Madame Phantasmagoria remained a mystery, as befitted the creator of astonishing delights.

The village was now free of expensive cars arriving so their owners could luxuriate in the hotel sauna, eat cordon bleu meals in its pretentious restaurant, and sunbathe round its marble-lined swimming pool. Wolf Enterprises' aspiration to attract wealth and celebrity dwindled into the realms of wishful thinking as the company teetered on the edge of bankruptcy. Will, Stuart and John had no choice but to accept the offer of a French business to buy them out. It didn't matter that the purchaser's portfolio was in entertainment. No one else was going to invest in the failed venture to make the village a playground for the rich and famous.

The signing of the agreement should have been a private affair, but the buyer insisted that it be public, in the parish hall.

The floor and gallery were packed with past and present villagers determined to see the local boys who had ruined their community suitably humiliated. When a stunningly attractive young woman representing the French company entered it made revenge even sweeter. Her clothes were stylish enough for an haute couture catwalk and beauty classical. Despite that, underneath it all, many of the locals thought that there was something familiar about those fine-looking features.

The young men facing financial ruin and investigation by the business regulator before their mid twenties were also unsettled by her presence. It was not only because they were about to sign their company over for a fraction of what it had cost to set up. When Will's father took the elegant woman's arm and escorted her to the desk where the contract was to be signed, it seemed like betrayal.

As she took ownership of their failed aspirations, there was no sign of triumph or smug satisfaction. It was enough that they knew her company managed many of the wealthy stars and VIPs they had aspired to attract.

After Will, Stuart and John drove away from the

village to plot their next crooked business venture there was a celebration in the crypt of the parish church. At its centre were Robyn and the elegant French woman who now held the future of the village in her immaculately manicured hands. No one, from vicar to the last surviving shopkeeper, seemed unduly bothered by this prospect and Ray, the community constable, had pieced together what had been going on. As soon he saw what had been stored down in the crypt, he knew for sure. Should he leave now before he became implicated in something he would be honour bound to report, or give in to terrible curiosity and discover how monstrous apparitions had undermined Wolf Enterprises?

The vicar blocked his retreat. "Meet the monsters of the fairway."

"But they're just marionettes..?" protested Ray. "Bloody good ones, but just puppets all the same."

"Something my old circus excels at," Robyn explained. "They could paralyse audiences with fright, or send them floating away in sheer delight. It's all smoke and mirrors, Ray. Or, in this case, lasers and projectors."

"But that can't be legal!"

"And who will prove it? Tomorrow the magician who breathed life into them will be on the other side of the Channel, spellbinding audiences with her astounding illusions."

"So what happens to the village now then? Who

owns us this time?"

"We do, dear fellow," said Will's father, "Which is more than any of us deserve. All the land my son's company bought and everything on it now belongs to the people of the parish."

"How?"

"Let's say that a bounteous angel invested wisely for us when she realised what was happening."

All eyes turned to the tall, elegant illusionist.

"Her stage name is Madame Phantasmagoria," announced Robyn, "but you may best remember her as Peony."

I'm On the Bus

Araminta lived life through her smartphone, gossiping to Chloe who lived on the other side of the world, Sandy only two doors away, and anyone and everyone in her address book. It would not be obesity or type two diabetes that took away this young life, it would be the lorry that ran her down while she was chatting on her phone.

Catching the bus for the regular weekend visit to her grandmother, Araminta had her smartphone pressed to her ear, listening to the inane banter of Penny who could speak without stopping for breath. Not being able to get a word in edgeways was frustrating.

At last Penny paused, giving her the chance to say, "I'm on the bus. Need to find my ticket. Got to go, Pen," and end the call.

Araminta dashed upstairs to the back seat where she called Ben who never interrupted. She often wondered if he listened to anything she said and was more absorbed with some computer game or other, slaying monsters or fending off invasions from heavily armed aliens. Ben was the only person she knew who could eat breakfast, talk on the phone, and hunt Pokémon at the same time. She could only wonder what he was doing by the time her bus stop came up - it was always best not to ask.

Araminta told him, "Got go now, Ben. This is my stop."

Her grandmother, Maisie, was busy as usual. In full-time work, she still had time to deliver weekend meals on wheels and run errands for elderly neighbours in the same block of flats. Araminta's visits were probably the only time she bothered to sit down.

They relaxed on the settee, looking out over the other blocks of flats, laundry flapping on balconies and pigeons cooing amorously on the safety railings. It was one of the few times Araminta was prepared to switch off her smartphone.

"Now what have you been up to, then?" Maisie asked.

Araminta wasn't sure what to say. When not chatting she was usually Googling gossip, watching the newest uploads on YouTube or listening to music. Her grandmother led a far more interesting life: she actually met the people in her circle of friends.

"Found this amazing new app which lets you link across social networks," Araminta told her.

"Sounds as though Facebook will soon put a stop to that. Aren't they rather possessive? I'm forever being bombarded with invitations to join them, but too old for that sort of thing."

That was just Maisie trying to sound her age. She was more savvy about the Internet than anyone else Araminta knew and far too grounded in reality to waste time chatting to people on the screen when she could just walk along the balcony or into the next street to see them.

"What was it like without the Internet and

mobile phones when you were young, Gran?" asked Araminta.

"Can't rightly remember now," said Maisie. "I was interested as soon as it was possible to do things on a word processor. When PCs and the Internet were available, writing a letter seemed very old-fashioned. Who knows, soon we will all email our Christmas cards because there won't be any stamps."

"Already do it with most of my friends. Brilliant cards out there - with animation and catchy tunes. Wouldn't send one to Mum, though. She still likes the real thing."

"I brought her up well."

"But she can't make liqueurs like yours."

Maisie recognised the hint. "Like to try my new one? It's a fusion of valerian and other herbs to help you relax."

Araminta could see how that would have been ideal for her overactive grandmother, but wasn't aware that she needed to calm down. The most exciting things in her life were online; dancing dogs, sneezing pandas and young men risking paraplegia by jumping into the sea from dangerously high rocks.

The valerian liqueur was sweet and highly flavoured to conceal the main ingredient, so Araminta swallowed it in one go before Maisie could warn her not to. Her granddaughter felt a soothing warmth surge through her body.

"Oh you silly little cow," muttered Maisie as she cursed herself for filling the glass too full.

When Araminta woke up it was lunch time. She

had promised to chat to Sophie on Skype at one: the satellite only allowed them 30 minutes so she didn't want to miss the connection and needed to get to her laptop.

Araminta kissed Maisie goodbye, snatched up her bag and dashed for the bus.

It was strangely empty for midday.

She took her usual seat upstairs at the very back and pulled out her smartphone.

Before she could decide who to call, half a dozen teenagers got on at the next stop.

They were unusually quiet and seemed to be floating.

Maisie's liqueur must have been stronger than Araminta thought because her surroundings started to take on a watery feel as the seats and the walls of the upper deck merged into a huge amoeba-like mattress. All the teenagers were bounced into a surreal dimension where the air buzzed with pixels trying to take on shapes without quite succeeding. There was something horribly fascinating about what they might have turned into... it could have been anything from a shower of frogs to herd of velociraptors.

Araminta tried to ask the others what was happening, but no words would come.

Her smartphone warbled its silly tune and she placed it to her ear.

"What did you say?" a voice asked.

"I said, 'Where are we?'"

"I dunno."

Araminta lowered the phone and tried to call out.

Again the words would not come. The other teenagers were pointing at their mobiles. This was the only way they could communicate.

During the panicked conversations, each of them started to change.

Their faces became rectangular, started to glow and were transformed into screens mirroring each owner's device. All they could do was look at their phones and see themselves desperately trying to claw their way out of them.

To her horror, Araminta realised that she was also trapped inside her smartphone. That device, her closest companion, had turned the teenager into a flickering anomaly that could be wiped from existence with one tap on the screen, or perhaps fade away as the battery drained.

Araminta could also see the screen faces of the other trapped teenagers, screaming to escape. From having the Internet at their fingertips, they were now part of the pantomime that had kept them entertained and were appearing in search results for the trivial and amusing. They were probably getting more hits than those minor celebrities stranded in the depths of some jungle the wildlife had deserted out of embarrassment.

For the first time in their lives, the trapped teenagers desperately needed the real world. Maisie's aversion to the trivia on the Internet now made sense. There were only so many times singing goats, nonentities behaving badly and idiots taking selfies on the edges of crumbling cliffs could be seen before the viewer started to wonder if life held a deeper meaning.

To make matters worse, the nightmare dimension that had engulfed them began to churn, whirling the teenagers and their phones round and round.

About them, all the silly selfies, would-be superstars and singing goats became bubbles of hot air which burst into oblivion.

Araminta's head was still spinning when something wet started to lick her face.

She woke with a screech.

"Stop that Wellington! Leave the girl alone!" Maisie's voice ordered.

Her neighbour's dopey Staffie leapt from the settee and dashed out onto the balcony to return to its home two doors up.

"Stupid dog. It's a wonder nobody's lodged a complaint about him."

"How long have I been asleep?" asked Araminta.

"Only half an hour. I didn't wake you because you looked as though you needed it. Bad dream?"

The teenager daren't tell her. Some nightmares are best forgotten.

Eyes in the Sky

As the flock of sheep munched the new shoots of grass moist with dew, they kept a wary eye on the weird creature that had come into their field yet again. It was scary and they wished it would go away. The hair protruding from the tight garment it wore was the shade of midnight and it kept glancing up apprehensively with purple eyes. The only things in the sky that bothered the sheep were crows, and other birds which swooped down to snatch beakfuls of wool to line their nests.

Donald's flock watched the strange creature push samples of grass and other forage into a flask, no doubt for a snack later, though everything about it indicated it would prefer a diet of raw meat. The furtive behaviour also suggested it was hiding from something else. It was unlikely to be Donald's sheep-dog. The shepherd was in his hut watching a film on an ancient laptop and there was no point in sending out Marchbanks. The dog was a toothless old collie that only recognised a sheep from three feet away. Goodness only knew what it would have made of the tall intruder in a suit that shimmered like petrol on water.

But help was on the way.

Here came little Daisy Dalziel. She would know what to do. She was very bright for a five-year-old and scared of nothing. And sure enough, she trotted over to the menacing creature and stood staring at it, hard. The flock of sheep backed away, bleating apprehensively, half expecting it to eat her. Instead the interloper stared back, short horns just visible as the dense hair parted when it threw back its head defiantly.

"You shouldn't be here. Donald doesn't like strangers in the same field as his sheep," Daisy admonished.

The creature put its head on one side and warbled with a strange melodic tone out of place coming from such a fearsome, fanged mouth.

"I will tell Parson Jamie and he will tell God," Daisy continued to scold. "The Devil has no right coming here."

The warble became high-pitched as though the visitor understood every word.

"You go away now," ordered Daisy and strode off to find out what film Donald was watching on his laptop.

Anyone older would have probably run for their life or had hysterics at encountering the demonic intruder, but this small island dweller was made of stern stuff.

"We should stop Marba secretly entering the experiment to collect all these samples," the Controller said. "Once these creatures realise that they are no longer on their own planet, all reaction will cease to be natural."

"At least that young specimen does not seem to be very concerned," agreed nes organiser. (Human gender pronouns do not apply to members of this species as they don't have different sexes.) "But we should really tell nem to come back in. Ne thinks we don't know what ne is doing. I know Marba has an interest in the vegetation of different planets, but this venture is too serious to waste time on green material."

Daisy reached the stone wall and turned just in time to see the strange creature fade from sight. She had come to expect it from this annoying trespasser. "I wish it wouldn't do that."

The five-year-old had been insisting that something strange was going on for weeks, but her parents and neighbours had put it down to an overactive imagination. However, the persistent nagging that they were not really where they thought they were was beginning to wear down their patience. Life was already hard enough on the remote island of their forebears; they didn't need an infant adding confusion to it. The sooner Daisy was packed off to school the better. Perhaps there she would learn to rein in her flights of fancy and stop describing horned beings that weren't goats, and seeing bat-like creatures circling the cliffs. Her most disturbing claim was that there were eyes everywhere, embedded in the rocks, peering out from the eaves of the community hall, and from the sky.

Her older brother, Thomas, was a much gentler soul who could not have dreamt up such dreadful things. Yet he still listened to his small sister as though she had wisdom lacking in older people. Perhaps their down-to-earth lives prevented them from seeing things they did not expect. Adults were like that and Daisy was not yet mature enough to know when to keep quiet.

"And they are up there, watching us all the time," Daisy whispered to Thomas when their parents couldn't hear.

"That's very silly, Daisy."

"Then tell me why you haven't been going to school?"

"Because the ferry hasn't been able to reach us." Thomas assumed that there was a very good reason and never enjoyed the crossing anyway, especially when the sea was rough. It would also be some time before the weather turned and they needed winter provisions. "Perhaps the engine is giving trouble? It is very old. And Mr Singh has enough groceries to keep the island supplied for weeks, so it probably doesn't matter too much."

"Of course it does, you stupid boy," Daisy scolded. "How do you expect to learn anything if you can't get to school? And Mr Singh's supplies should have run out long ago, but nobody seems to wonder where the new ones are coming from. There aren't any other ferries and we would have heard a helicopter."

Thomas was beginning to understand why the way Daisy saw things so worried the adults. It was as though everyone above the age of seven had been inoculated against noticing the obvious, but he was too afraid to believe his young sister's insistence that something was wrong. Knowing that Daisy was an honest child with a vivid imagination, yet would never lie, worried him.

"That child has awareness beyond normal for her species," Marba insisted.

"That is why the research will be ruined if the others start to believe her, and all the more reason you should keep away," warned the Controller.

"Perhaps we can talk to her?"

"And tell her what? Aliens have transported her island to another planet to monitor the mentality of a species which could be dangerous if it ever manages to travel into space?"

"The Ruling Council insists it must be done. Humans cannot be let loose in the Galaxy until their reaction to stress has been assessed," added the organiser. This child may not be alarmed by an alien, but the older of her species could behave differently. The only way to test their reactions without endangering ourselves is to measure what they do in an unexpected catastrophe."

"Your small friend cannot be there when it happens," insisted the Controller.

"But Daisy is only an infant," Marba protested.

"And they are the most perceptive. The members of this species stop seeing clearly as they grow older and only comprehend things as they want them to be. That is why they could be dangerous."

Observations of larger human communities had been inconclusive and complicated by too many other factors. The only problem in this remote island community was Daisy. She might work out that her island had been temporarily replaced by a replica to prevent raising the suspicions of the outside world. The researchers could not take the risk of the adults believing her.

Daisy was reading a book with one hand and combing her teddy bear's fur with the other.

Suddenly she was no longer in front of the stove in the farmhouse scullery. This new place was airy and bright, and filled with people like the interloper she scolded whenever she saw it. And they all made that strange warbling noise.

Daisy, still clutching her teddy and book, stretched to her full height of almost three and a half feet. "Why can't you speak properly? It's very rude to do that."

59

"Ignore her," the Controller told the others. "Just start the experiment."

Marba disregarded the order and warbled at the five-year-old, "Everything is alright, Daisy. It will be over soon."

To her amazement, Daisy could understand the alien. "What are you going to do?"

The Controller had no idea that young humans needed to be humoured. "This trial will determine whether your species shall be confined to its planet for perpetuity."

"What's that?" she demanded.

"Forever," Marba explained.

"Strange creatures like you shouldn't use long words."

"This isn't really helping us come to a decision," Marba quietly chided.

Daisy didn't like the sound of that so decided to keep quiet. She took her teddy over to a large window and looked down on her island. It was no longer in the middle of a cold, deep sea in Earth's northern hemisphere. The horizon surrounding it boiled like the surface of the sun, only it was intense blue. Daisy already knew that her people hadn't really been where they thought they were, but she hadn't expect-ed this.

She squealed in fright.

"It's all right, nobody will be hurt," Marba reas-sured her, "Everything will soon return to normal and you won't remember this ever happened."

The alien's soft warbling tone did not comfort the five-year-old as the sky above the island merged with the sky and became a curtain of roiling fury, threatening to shed liquid rage on its inhabitants.

Daisy's mother was leading the search party frantically searching for her young daughter. She had to be found before the storm came. Having always lived on the island, she knew everything the elements could throw at it. Those not searching brought in the flocks and ensured the children and elderly were safe in the solid-walled kirk. The strong roof which had weathered hundreds of storms was their best protection. Parson Jamie encouraged his congregation to join in prayer for the deliverance of the lost child and their survival while the elements churned into a tempest even JM Turner would have found it difficult to paint

The Controller was puzzled by the islanders' stoical reaction. "What are they doing?"

"They call it praying," explained Marba. "These beings believe in supreme deities that have created and control all things. Others use this conviction called religion as an excuse to slaughter each other."

"This is not what I had expected."

"Isolated as they are, how else could they react?" Marba chided.

The Controller recalled the vegetation lover's

original objection to using this small community for their research, but its isolation had been too convenient. It would have been impossible to relocate a larger, land-locked population where reactions were more likely to represent human nature.

"Why didn't you mention this thing called religion before?"

"I wasn't aware of their beliefs until Daisy mistook me for this Devil, the entity they regard as the evil opposition to her God."

The Controller realised the futility of the test. "Stop the experiment."

The soft warbling of the team fell silent.

It was broken by Daisy's piercing voice, "You don't know much, do you?"

Being exposed to the environment of the alien observation centre had enhanced the five-year-old's understanding to that of an adult's. Daisy hardly knew where the words were coming from, only that they made terrible sense.

"The people on my island would never turn on each other - that's what you expected them to do, wasn't it?"

"We need to measure how stress triggers conflict amongst your species," explained Marba.

"Then look at the rest of the world - not us!" Daisy snapped. "We're not guinea pigs!"

"The catastrophes it would be necessary to trigger on a much larger population are proscribed," the

Controller was obliged to explain.

"There are already disasters happening, and most of them caused by people. Why do you need to experiment on us?"

"It is the only alternative we have to the opinion of an expert who knows your species well. We have been unable to find one."

Daisy stamped petulantly. "Well, if I tell you that humans should never be allowed into space until they grow up, would that be expert enough for you?"

"But you are a human. Why would you do that?"

"Because on our island we can see the rest of the world for what it is. That's why we like it where we are."

Daisy suddenly woke from a strange dream. She was by the scullery stove clutching her book and teddy bear. The sun was setting and in the distance the local ferry could be seen on the horizon, sailing towards the island on a calm sea.

Her mother and brother were fast asleep in the parlour armchairs, so she put on her coat to help Donald bring the sheep into their fold. Marchbanks, his old collie, was no longer much help and Donnie, the new sheepdog, was too fond of nipping their legs and needed to be trained up more.

It transpired that the rest of the island had also suffered from the sleeping sickness, though soon recovered. It was a relief to have the ferry back so Mr

Singh could stock up his groceries. Then, when it was no longer able to reach them, they would be cushioned from the rest of the tumultuous world.

The remote community watched the warning being broadcast to the whole planet from outer space. It hardly seemed important.

No one on the island wanted to travel into the Galaxy and colonise other worlds anyway.

Game Over

"Online... Connected... Game Running..."

Danny entered the code he had downloaded, selected an avatar, and started to play.

The dragon had long ceased to be fearsome. Its faded golden flanks were chipped and scratched, and the wooden flames from its nostrils all but knocked off by numerous collisions with the safety barrier. As roller coasters went, this should have been a health and safety hazard. Many modern rides were ten times as scary, taking their riders virtually into the stratosphere, upside down, and with centrifugal forces only astronauts experienced. The modest height of this track was reassuring and promised a trauma free trip while the dire state of its maintenance threatened sudden death.

The roller coaster belonged to Jacob's Amazing Funfair, which was full of rickety rides and side stalls inviting sharpshooters to try their luck using rifles with misaligned sites, or knock down coconuts with wooden balls hard enough to fracture the skull of an elephant. Small wonder it had not appeared before. It was probably trying to avoid the authorities who would close it down as a danger to public health.

Howie, Donnie, Sabrina and Annie were horribly fascinated. No travelling funfair had ever dared pitch its rides on this marshy meadow before.

The young adults decided to try shooting the

rotating ducks first. Tokens were handed to the stall holder who promptly stepped out of line of fire further than was necessary. Sabrina was the most competitive, and furious that the ducks swerved aside when she knew full well that her pellets should have hit them.

Frustration soon set in, so the friends decided to try the ancient swingboats. When they took their seats they wobbled unnervingly and as soon as Donnie and Annie tugged the ropes their boats took off as though trying to loop the loop. The scary experience jolted forward the inexplicable thought that they been here before. But that was impossible... surely?

As soon as the attendant stopped the boats with the braking ropes, the friends leapt out. Sabrina was predictably annoyed at having her hair mussed. She was not experiencing the same feeling of déjà vu as the others, but reluctantly followed them to the roundabout of horses with manic looks in their eyes.

The ride should have been safe enough for infants, with mounts that only gently dipped and rose at a moderate speed, so they climbed aboard. As soon as they did so the eyes of the prancing horses lit up and the roundabout spun so fast the companions were thrown off onto the sodden grass.

The others only just managed to persuade Sabrina not to storm off.

Perhaps she was right and it was time to leave, but that sense of déjà vu held Howie, Donnie and Annie in its thrall. If they did nothing else, they knew they had to ride the roller coaster. The state of its dilapidated dragon carriage and rotten tracks should have told them that it wasn't a good idea. Sabrina loudly protested that it wasn't safe but, too afraid to be left on her own, stepped into it all the same.

As they plunged down the first dip the companions screeched with the obligatory euphoria, which immediately turned to terror when the buckled track reared up and pointed them heavenwards. They were shot into the sky, clinging desperately to the safety bars of the dragon car as they entered Earth's orbit.

It was then Sabrina disappeared.

Danny's screen flashed 'GAME OVER' triumphantly as the program announced that its creator it had defeated the user.

"This game is rubbish!" he groaned. "What a waste of time. Whoever wrote it really needs to get a life."

The dragon roller coaster carriage continued in its orbit. As Howie, Donnie and Annie gazed at the radiant planet below everything flooded back.

Now they knew what they were doing there.

"We made it then!" Howie should not have sounded so surprised.

"It was inevitable someone would play it eventually," Annie said.

"Just as well they never reached the coconut shy and won - our minds could have been wiped."

Donnie hardly dare believe what Howie had just

said. "You have to be joking? Writing this software is one thing, but sodding around with our brains is another."

"I'm sure there wasn't any danger of that," Annie tried to persuade herself.

"And how do we get back? You did include an escape hatch - didn't you?"

"The electrodes should have cut out when the game ended. I don't understand how we got trapped here." There was an edge of panic in Howie's voice.

"You designed the interactive program so we could enter it. You tell us why they didn't."

"I knew it wasn't a good idea to upload that demo. We should have listened to Sonnie."

"You know she would have stopped us."

"Wish she had," whimpered Annie.

"You knew that as soon as some kid decided to play it we risked being up stuck here!" raged Donnie.

"Bet he was really pissed off."

Xing, known as Sonnie, returned from lunch to see her three young techs sitting stock still and staring blankly at their monitors. She had only been gone for an hour, yet during that time they had managed to send their minds to some electronic la-la land. This was the trouble with giving kids with too much talent for their own good a free rein. They would have been safer in GCHQ who could provide better supervision than her agency.

Sonnie could have pulled the electrodes from their tousled heads and hoped for the best, or just terminated the program. Neither option was a good idea. There was only one thing for it.

She picked up the spare headset, attached the electrodes to her head and entered the program.

Reality took a nose dive and dropped her into the dilapidated roller coaster carriage from Jacob's Amazing Funfair. It was immediately obvious that Howie, Donnie and Annie were having anything but fun. This had to be Howie's work: a mind that hovered between elation, hallucination and depths of despair. After this he was definitely seeing that therapist.

The techs had hardly dared hope their superior would try to rescue them, but there she was, perched on the dragon's head in the carriage orbiting the Earth.

"Okay, you've all proved what smartarses you are. Next time remember where you put the exit code."

They all turned to Howie. He looked uncomfortable.

"You can remember where it is, can't you?"

The young tech fidgeted uneasily. "It's like this, you see..."

"Oh, for pity's sake!" exclaimed Annie. "The dork's forgotten."

"I bet Alan Turing never had this problem," agreed Donnie.

"Alan Turing didn't have to work with twits like him."

"I know it's somewhere in this carriage," Howie

prevaricated.

"If we ever manage to get back, you're relegated to writing software for local government schemes to save frogs," Sonnie promised. "That equipment belongs in the hands of neuroscientists, not inept adolescents."

The young people muttered various subdued, "Sorrys", "Won't happen agains", and "We'll sort it..." promises.

"I know!" Howie suddenly recalled. "Pull the dragon's beard!"

Without a word, Sonnie reached out of the carriage and yanked the decaying wood.

Panic set in as they hurtled towards the Earth.

As soon as they had crashed back to reality they snatched off the electrodes glued to their heads.

Silence ensued for some time. The screensavers on their monitors kicked in and they watched bubbles and morphing boxes through monstrous headaches.

Only Howie could have asked after that experience. "Think we should patent it, boss?"

Butterflies

Christopher Lovelace had only one ambition.

Older and wiser heads knew that he was being unrealistic, but saw no sense in discouraging a worthy aspiration in one so young.

And where could be the harm in growing a meadow full of wild flowers to attract butterflies?

His Great Uncle Frank was quite happy to let the eight-year-old have that small patch of land impossible to cultivate because of its poor soil and lack of access due to some ancient oak trees. The Victorian owner of the estate had used it to build an ice house. That had been reduced to rubble over the years. Removing it would probably be beyond the strength of the delicate Christopher, but if the boy wanted to attract the butterflies, who was Great Uncle Frank to argue. During the time the old man had been farming the land, their numbers had dwindled and it was now unusual to see just one.

It was also much healthier for his great-nephew to be outdoors rather than tapping away at a computer or smartphone, chatting to others of his age with no ambitions. Christopher's parents may have lived in a cottage on the farm, but they had no interest in the land. They had dwindled into technology's children, working from home on the infernal devices their Uncle Frank had only contempt for, even if they did bring in more income than the farm could ever hope to. They never seemed to have time for their clever little son. The child needed to be outside, building up his strength to help the ancient Cuthbert when he could no longer lift the buckets of feed for the pigs or muck out their pens. Christopher could already cope with the farmyard smell that made that stuck-up mother of his feel faint. His genes came from Great Uncle Frank's side of the family and the old man was going to be damned before the farm was passed on to a nephew whose idea of an honest day's work was gazing at a laptop screen.

Christopher's mother suspected that Great Uncle Frank had put the idea of the butterfly meadow into her son's head. Six months before he had been a quiet seven-year-old too timid to weed the flowerboxes for fear of finding worms. Now the child who used to shriek at the sight of a caterpillar wanted to plant a meadow to encourage butterflies. As far as she knew none of Christopher's friends had any interest in insects; one or two probably didn't even know what they were. His obsession had started after the twins from a nearby farm stopped playing with him near the old outhouses. They had soon lost interest in chasing each other through the dilapidated buildings, unable to deal with the mud and stench of manure that pervaded the yard. The twins came from a clinically clean, automated farm where machinery milked the cows and cleaned up the slurry in the huge sheds that housed them. Eight-year-olds were certainly not allowed inside those.

Great Uncle Frank had wondered if Christopher's fascination with butterflies had been encouraged at school where nature study was just as important as reading and writing, but then began to wonder if there was another reason.

One day he saw Christopher talking to a slightly built girl in the rubble strewn piece of land he intended to transform into a wild meadow. The farmer's first impulse was to find out who the older girl was, then thought again. Christopher was a sensible young boy, and there would have been no point in breaking up what was, quite probably, an innocent exchange. The girl, dressed in a frock of delicate pastel shades which fluttered like butterfly wings, looked far too inoffensive to harm a child anyway. Great Uncle Frank stood and watched to be on the safe side until Christopher's companion appeared to dissolve away into the overhanging leafy branches of an oak tree. That told him he should really get his eyes tested again.

Christopher saw his great uncle and waved happily. The eight-year-old was obviously delighted after meeting the girl, and the farmer could only wonder what they had been discussing. Then, as usual, the small boy busied himself pulling loose bricks from the ground and carrying them, one by one, to the border of the meadow to construct a rough wall. Uncle Frank could see that it would take forever, but his great nephew was very independent and might be offended if he sent one of the farm hands over to help. No, the family came from the school of hard knocks and he decided it would help toughen up the boy.

Christopher carried on working until dusk when his mother came over to take him home. He had to go to school the next day and needed to get to bed early.

In the morning, as the sun rose the, girl Christopher had been talking to appeared in the meadow. She waved to Cuthbert, the elderly farm hand, on his early morning rounds to feed the pigs. Dog walkers were not unusual at that time of day, so he waved back.

As he reached the pig pens, Cuthbert turned to see a vibrant rainbow flickering over the butterfly meadow. He put down the bucket of swill to stand and gaze. That was no rainbow; it was light being reflected off thousands of fluttering wings. At their centre, Christopher's friend became infused with iridescent colours and opened huge wings as frail as tissue paper.

Cuthbert fainted.

When the farmhand came round he was gazing up at a sky filled with shimmering wings. Christopher was dancing through the meadow in the early sun, swirls of the bright insects looping about him like chiffon streamers.

Cuthbert convinced himself he was dreaming,

closed his eyes and fell asleep where he had fallen. He was still snoring on the ground when the cows were driven back from the pasture to be milked. Until then everyone believed he had done his rounds and left for the pub. It was assumed that he had suffered one of his turns. The medicine he washed down with a pint of ale meant that it was a regular occurrence; one of the reasons he was not allowed to drive a tractor.

The doctor declared that there was nothing wrong with Cuthbert a few weeks holiday couldn't cure and, considering his age of 86, he had probably been overdoing it. Great Uncle Frank had known him all his life and knew Cuthbert had never overdone anything unless it involved a bribe of ale or prod with a sharp stick.

The old farm hand didn't mention what he had seen in the meadow that morning: hallucinating at his age meant being assessed for dementia. For all he knew, he might fail the tests.

Several years passed. The butterflies swarmed to Christopher's meadow and the government schemes for farmers to set aside land for wildlife encouraged other dwindling species to reclaim their natural habitats.

The child who loved butterflies grew into a delicate young man, too frail to attend college. He had still been at school when the doctor sent him for tests to find out why the son of a farming family was not growing into a sturdy youth. The specialist explained that it was a condition of the blood when Christopher was within earshot. When he wasn't, she used the word leukaemia, believing it would be better explained to him by his parents.

Christopher took the news well, as though he had not expected to spend long in this world. And it meant that he could to spend all his time in the meadow his late Great Uncle Frank had bequeathed him in his will and watch the butterflies feeding from the buddleia, scabious and knapweed. As the caterpillars of the previous year emerged from their chrysalises with jewelled wings, it was a delight to see such unlikely insects being transformed into something so wonderful.

One afternoon Christopher did not return home. There was panic amongst family and friends who feared the worse. Surely he would have phoned if unable to walk back by himself. But when they searched, all that they found in the meadow was his mobile phone and sketchpad. It was unlike Christopher to disappear this way. He had never wandered off before without telling someone.

Given his weak condition, the young man couldn't have gone far, yet no trace of him was ever found.

Summer turned to autumn and autumn turned to winter. It was only then his family accepted that they would probably never see him again. Although Christopher's illness was terminal, it was still hard to have no remains to bury or ashes to scatter over his beloved butterfly meadow.

So family and friends gathered there on the anniversary of his disappearance to unveil a plaque to his memory.

As they formed a circle about it something large pushed its way up through the spring flowers. It was a large, iridescent chrysalis filled with a radiant glow. It began to dissolve and a slender girl with huge, gossamer wings appeared directly above the gathering.

A marvellous butterfly burst from the chrysalis.

With one downbeat of shimmering wings, it joined its companion in the sky.

The huge butterflies briefly circled above the watching group in farewell, and then faded into the dappled sunlight.

"That was the young woman I saw Christopher with that day!" exclaimed Cuthbert.

As he was now well into his nineties and ale dependent, he would not have been believed if someone else had not declared,

"And that was Christopher with her!"

CPSIA information can be obtained
at www.ICGtesting.com
Printed in the USA
LVOW10s1626040118
561818LV00029B/831/P